Four Walks

by

Simon Ross

Simon Ross was born in Reigate in Surrey in 1973. He moved with his family to Ayr on the west coast of Scotland in 1983. He graduated with a degree in history of art and film studies from Glasgow University and then spent the next 20 years working in finance. In 2015 he moved to Macclesfield , Cheshire where he began performing at poetry events and releasing self produced poetry collections. In 2022 he achieved a masters degree with distinction in creative writing from Salford University and was recipient of the Leanne Bridgewater award . He currently works as a community therapist for the NHS. 4 Walks is his first published long form work.

FOUR WALKS

A collection of poetry,

short stories and an essay on Poetics

by Simon Ross

ISBN: 978-1-7391474-7-1
Independent Publishing

Alien Rabbit Limited
www.alienrabbit.co.uk

Contents

"I
watched
it
slip
away"

Atrocity Exhibition (1980)

17.07.22

It was only as I was getting ready to leave and scrolling through my Facebook feed that I realised the significance of the date. A picture of Ian Curtis appeared on the screen of my phone. Unusually it was in colour, he was wearing a red shirt, framed against a black background, face pale, caught in the stage lights.

The accompanying text explained it was his birthday and that he would have been 62 today. This jolted me. I had arranged to meet Aitch today to walk through the streets of Macclesfield to try to understand something of Curtis, his relationship with the town and my own understanding of the person and the place. The date had been selected from a choice of three possibilities and today was the one that best fitted with other commitments. As I walked the 20 minute journey to the rendezvous point I couldn't decide if this chronological synchronicity was auspicious or in some way damaging to the albeit sketchy premise that by walking and talking our way through the town, knowledge, or something close to it could be revealed.

this was not

it was unintentional

does this align more thoroughly

or

create

dissonance

a sentimental journey

into the past that locates in the present

indications towards a future

on foot towards the journey on foot

does one end as one begins/it's all walking

pandemic nostalgia for empty skies and birdsong/ now it is just another risk

the other that makes the task a quest

ixat god of transit on dog day morning

dressing for the job we did not apply for

by not disclosing a plan a plan emerges

hovering by the fake we make it real by acknowledging the absence of authenticity it becomes its own sign

midlife fork and knife choice (there was no choice) becoming the axis of exchange

Aitch had messaged me the previous evening, relaying that he had just recovered from a bout with covid. He said he was left with a "brain fog and a poor sense of direction". This corresponded well with my position as an unreliable navigator with an indistinct idea that needed both a witness and a collaborator to propel the speculation into something more tangible.

We met by the taxi rank in front of the station, it was a flat grey sky morning, the air was warm. We both wore boots for walking and carried rucksacks. I had been deliberately and unavoidably vague in our prior exchanges as to the purpose of the jaunt. As we made our way along Sunderland Street I filled in the details such as they were.

We were paused outside a bookshop that had opened in the month prior to the pandemic, lurched through various lockdowns and the occasional reopening's and then sputtered out in the resumption of normality. During its brief existence in the book trade, the shop had

biblio arbitrageur in catastrophic epoch resolves to exit / no protocol for this exists

deconstruct window dressed texts left outside indifferent to deferral of meaning

sell the idea and vanish before the foundations are laid / speculate on future myth cycles /keep opaque accounts /always unavailable for comment – supplement

in the clearing something is revealed not discovered

always already started

there was no other option open

52.25807°N, 2.12562°W

"walk to Macclesfield, then

bus" 3.2.36 , Orwell diaries

26.1.63 Beatles play El Rio - "Please, please me" released 15 days previously

Where are we George

Nowhere man

specialised in slightly worn, overpriced paperbacks. A conversation with the proprietor revealed they had inherited a vast library from a relative and this had prompted them to quit an unforgiving career in academia and strike out as a bookseller. I would pay a visit whenever I passed and generally walk out with a purchase that I could have found at a fraction of the price online. It was the sheer audacity of opening a second hand bookshop that kept me coming back, the crazed recklessness, the horrendous timing, the stoic ability to overcharge and not blink.

In its lifetime the establishment had been literary in pretensions with an eye for the unusual cover and the early edition. These days in its afterlife as an abandoned enterprise the window was an array of Maeve Binchy, Catherine Cookson, Jeffrey Archer. This was a ghost shop, doors padlocked, and the electricity cut off. The old stock cleared, repackaged in boxes, sent back to a storage facility somewhere of the M62. What had emerged was the idea of a bookshop, the notion that books were for sale in the town outside of the charity shops and the ubiquitous Waterstones. It had the feel of a marketing strategy to suggest the bohemian possibilities of place, property developer semiology indicating the concept rather than the reality of something happening here that you really couldn't afford to miss.

As we took in the stage paste suggestion of culture, the mock up for a proto Hay on Wye of the north west, I divulged what I could of the itinerary. We would perambulate across the urban environment pausing at five preordained points to contemplate the significance that they held as locations in the life story of Ian Curtis. Aitch gracefully nodded ascent, we strode on to our point of entry, our point of departure.

The Mural – Mill Street adjacent to the Bus Station.

George Orwell had been here before us. In a brief mention in the diaries that form a companion piece to The Road to Wigan Pier he describes catching a bus to Manchester from the bus station in Macclesfield. There is no description in the text, no analysis, just a mechanical fact noted, as connective tissue in a broader body of inquiry. Except he hadn't. In the 1930's the bus station had been a few hundred yards north of here, where the medical centre now stands, a stone's throw from the now vanished El Rio theatre where the Beatles played in 1963.

We muse on the spectral
Georges, Orwell and Harrison in
ethereal collision, flickering in a
time vortex in the concourse of
the surgery carpark.

We take in the mural like good
tourists. It's a blow up of a classic
Kevin Cummins photograph.
Curtis's wedding ring Is
prominent, his gaze is beatific.
The image is fixed on a gable end
above a convenience store that
advertises they only accept cash.

Aitch remarks upon the idea that
the town can now bathe in the
reflected glory of the iconic
image as if they themselves
become legendary through
association. A few days later I
am watching a film of the
unveiling ceremony on you tube
and realise he is not wrong. The
assembled crowd all look happy
to be there, perhaps somehow
relieved that the image
correlates to a recognisable
collective memory of the singer.
There is no conceptual
interpretation necessary, this is
not difficult art on a formal level.
It reinforces rather than
challenges any preconceptions.

We meander away from the site
and up the slope of Mill Street. I

Image punctures townscape
/time fixed from a short time
left/ looking upward and away
/beyond

Here is the icon, each day /day
in day out/ an easy decode for
the casual stroller/ place unites
in image / the mayor cut the
ribbon in the sun/ clapping/
and phone cameras

Being dragged by unforeseen
gravity, proposals rewritten by
circumstance/ things not in the
script become the narrative,
pace drops, long still shots,
people sitting watching being
watched

"she is leaving" coin falls
amongst a scattering of
coins/troubadour eats for
another day The intersection of
the walk and the destination,
folds in the journey/ always
something else. A contingent
location /adjacent, unexpected

Contemplating the possibility
of failure in the medieval. It
wouldn't have worked
then/there either Fresco/ fiasco
of establishing connections as
justification, mild road fever,
hallucinating possibility, letting
things be as they are is time set
adrift

soon realise a flaw in my proposed method. Aitch is absorbed in the street architecture stalling to examine drain covers and window frame sashes. He comments on the

stationary seated observers of the urban promenade, he is immersed in the quotidian, the civic everyday. A busker strums lightly and croons "she's leaving home" Aitch is deeply attentive and visibly moved. I tithe the singer with the change in my pocket, an offering to enable our transit to the next node on our route. It occurs to me that the in between is as significant as the destinations, perhaps whatever is to be revealed will become clear in the spaces that define and contrast the focal points of our journey.

We gain the high ground of the market square and contemplate the blackened stone exterior of St Michaels Church. It feels rude not to drop in and absorb the 14th century Chapel. As we stand amongst the sleeping effigies and medieval stained glass, I resort to pseudo tour guide mode recalling there had been unconfirmed speculation that an anchoress had dwelt in the structure and had ultimately been walled up when she gave up the ghost. I relate the tale perhaps to assuage the sense that this is not strictly Curtis space and we are deviating into centreless derive. In my head I head I construct the faux notion that the anchoress' fate translates well into the enwalling in paint of the singer on the gable end on MIll Street. Fixed within architecture they radiate a place memory both unstable, uncertain.

Back on the trail we drift up King
Edward Street. On another day I
would have regaled Aitch with
the tales of Bonnie Prince
Charlie occupying the town
briefly in 1745 and residing in a
building on the corner and then
reminded him that Cromwell
stopped at the Bate Hall pub
further along street during the
civil war. But not today. We are
dowsing for another ghost.

"Every corner abandoned too soon"

Atmosphere (1979)

On the corner of Chestergate we
come across an unsolicited
image of the quarry. A stencil and
spray paint screenshot from a
film four decades old. It captures
Curtis in an incipient St Vitus
rapture. Paint drips and the
fading texture of the outline
suggest a presencing and a
disappearance. The piece is
signed CKING. Seeking, but for
what and can a shade be sought
and if it were found , what then?

The ethics of our walking seance
preoccupy us as we make our
way to the junction at Katherine
Street. We are out of the
commercial district and into the
domestic. Rows of two up to

Path regained, no time for scant
detail of a history misread,
muttered reminisces
inappropriate to the quest
must be shunned

Thinking about the stencil
being cut by hand in a
house/the spray paint
purchased. Both placed in a bag
and taken to the wall, in the
pre-dawn, of empty streets, the
rattle and hiss of the can /
signed / Poseidon

Urban transition zone
/work/live/place triangulating,
corners leaking

*"the crown belongs to the
philanthropic manufacturers of
the Macclesfield silk district.
They employed the youngest
children of all, even from five to
six years of age" Engels*

53.25359⁰ N 2.13188⁰ W

Seeking an emotion for the
anonymity of locale.
Anticlimax to a (life)climax

Blank (________) generation of
affect (less)

Expectations diminishing

down terraces that housed the Mill workers that shouldered the growth of the town out of the agrarian and into the industrial.

Engels had been another big name erstwhile navigator of the area. He notes the terrible working conditions and child labour that underwrote the dizzy transformation of time and place wrought by the factory and the machine.

The House

We negotiate the grids and backcourts of the street network arriving at the corner of Barton Street. I draw our walk to a halt at no.77. The place where Curtis died.

Aitch is underwhelmed. He reflects on the UPVC door with the red roses inlaid in the glass. The mundane repetition of the brickwork, the anonymity of the architecture. Just another house in just another street like so many others. It's as if the building has been reconfigured to resist memorial, to decline pilgrimage. Averting one's eyes seems the only acceptable response. The non pull, a gravity that repels.

A few days later, researching after the event, I land upon an estate agents site that handled the transaction for a recent sale of the property. The blurb describes it as "a double fronted character cottage" with an asking

Baudelaire/Blavatsky erratic ectoplasm, stalling for time, the psychic investigator sighs

Janus/ the face polarised extending both and neither

Either will offer a betrayal

Michel Certeau

Asyndeton - the ellipsis of conjunctive loci

Mistaking pilgrimage for illumination, we tell stories to confuse ourselves into belief

53.25427° N 2.13082° W

Bets hedged in civil service torpor if rock and roll dream fades

Exploded star memory

Elusive desire reconciliation (MIA) instability of the reproductive sign

Always the inbetween, the unmarked, the speechless, can it speak

price of £115K. Double fronted seems to define our activity and our person of interest. As walkers through someone else's past we are unreliable. Part flaneur part table tapper. The image of Curtis that we have seen, that is fixed, is only a shadow, a darkroom facsimile of a life lived, however brief.

"The long poem of walking manipulates spatial organisations"

"To walk is to lack a place"

We edge away, awed at the everyday blankness. Any significance is projected by us on to the location. It refuses to offer up theories or to decipher complexities, we accept the invitation to move away from the nothing to see.

The Labour Exchange

Around the corner we are immediately in a place more amenable to our need to excavate legend, refocus memory and dream speculatively. We are at the labour exchange, where the singer and lyricist worked during the formative phase of Joy Division's existence.

The building is marked by the only other public memorial to Curtis. A round marble black plaque inscribed "1978_1979" below a reproduction of the Unknown Pleasures album cover fixed high above head height on a chocolate brown brick wall. Aitch takes exception to the underscore utilised in the date line, the loaded eschewal of the conventional hyphen. He feels the presence of the designer Peter Saville looming over the composition. Curtis has been elided by design, this is a memory device of /for another artist, the tribute excludes the subject from the scene.

The building itself has been transformed into housing. Again, the Curtis myth trail is translated into property speculation, labour exchanged for rest. The doorways are inscribed above the lintel, MEN WOMEN INFANTS. There are two masculine portals, an indication of the scale of the temporary idling of the millworkers who found themselves spasmodically rendered surplus to requirements as the price of silk oscillated from boom to bust.

We drift downstream, the road undulates, slopes and falls. Aitch draws attention to the wild grasses and flowers sprouting abundantly from the cracks in the flagstones and kerbs.

"sous les paves le champ"

 He pauses and stoops to reposition a scattering of stones and places a vacated snail shell carefully to complete the subtle recomposing of this "unofficial countryside."

 Wabi sabi – the three marks of existence / sanobin, impermanence; mujo, suffering; ku, emptiness/absence of self-nature. The act fits as well as any other in the bid to let the life of Curtis reanimate through considered maintenance of place.

"A point of view creates more waves"

Autosuggestion (1979)

The street feels like a punctum in the flow of the perambulation. A time stoppage, the pavements are empty, a gentle breeze is blowing. The atmosphere recalls a holiday excursion away from the main resort, where unfamiliar territory is made mysterious by mapless navigation.

We next encounter an ice cream factory, Granelli's. Impossible to resist, we enter into the shop, after some minutes observing the museum of ancient dairy churns and street vendors carts. In crossing the threshold, we step back into 1950. A neatly dressed girl at the counter with her hair firmly tied back invites us to peruse the multiplicity of flavours on offer. We both opt for pistachio. The counter girl informs us that they have no card machine. I reach into my pocket and offer the change garnered from the water stop below the mural, diminished by the offering to the busker but still more than enough to cover the cost.

Back outside we consume our green frozen food. A brief sensory return to the children we were when the stark, brief drama of Curtis' life unfolded.

Onward and we descend from the slopes to the flatlands around Christchurch. Built in 1793 by silk magnate Charles Roe with an interior to hold 1400 souls, a capacious Victorian graveyard, and a rumoured medieval plague pit. The building, whose tower, is visible for miles from the approach roads to the town, has recently reincarnated as a music venue. Curtis' old bandmate, the bassist Peter Hook had played there with his band the Light a month previously. The group resurrecting the Joy Division catalogue a few hundred yards from the room the lyrics to the songs were written.

"the shadow that stood by the side of the road"

Komakino (1980)

We find ourselves examining a row of derelict cottages on Shaw Street one of three thoroughfares that converge on the east side of the church. We must have been recast in the urban theatre of our procession, without being privy to the script as a passer by inquires

"Are you property developers?"

We look at one another sheepishly and consider the accuracy of the stranger's assessment. Yes and no. We have no capital to stake on the burgeoning gentrification vison however we are investing our imaginations in the unknown potentials of place, we speculate in undefined possibilities, the alchemy of place dreams, building care homes for ghosts.

Ultimately we dissemble and plead civilian status. Two adults out on a weekday afternoon stroll in the civic hinterland, purposeful in our purposelessness. *Creatively doing nothing."*

"that's a pity, that rows been empty for years"

We discuss the contradiction of inaction on the site that is both desirably located and retentive of a heritage charm, the industrial domestic awaiting net zero smart home renovation.

Time and space reunite

Missing the protagonist

Recognised in the act of transformation/ In the transformational, A skin sloughed is left as evidence / past /passed/lives

Performative art practice, misread by the accidental audience/ the ambiguity of intent/ reality will always, is always waiting- beware!

Lacking conviction, we miss the truth, spread the inaccuracies further/ entropy unfolds / irreversibly

"Iain Sinclair"

Nominee accounts, shell structures. A brass plate in a post-colonial archipelago / an answer machine that clicks on/off.

"there's something not right about it. I can't even find out who owns it."

They speculate on underhand planning administration at the council offices before striding off and away from the reforgotten terraced row.

Time, that had fallen out of joint in our fugue walk, clicks back into place and I summon the energy to lead on to the next significant location.

"Pulled in close by the buildings side

In a group all forgotten youth

Had to think"

Interzone (1978)

The Kings School has been present on the site, now bordering a busy roundabout on Westminster Road, since 1502. Curtis had attended, as had the Joy Division drummer Stephen Morris.

It was perhaps this robust, classically inflected educational regime that elevated Curtis's lyrics above the fractured slogans and jump cut assemblages that defined the verbal output of his post punk contemporaries.

Aitch is resonating as we peer through the iron gates. Members of his family were old boys; their time served a decade in advance of the spectral avatar we haplessly pursue.

He recalls playing schoolboy cricket on the pitch that foregrounds the neo gothic buildings arranged around the perimeter of the outfield.

Once again we are witnessing the translation of property, the shift from the socially utilitarian to an item in a speculative portfolio. The cricket green is swathed in waist high grasses and the schoolrooms are obscured in the scaffolding and heavy load transportation of the construction industry.

The school itself morphed and reconfigured a few miles up the road in 2020 to the premiership footballers haven of Prestbury. The ex site hovers in developmental limbo with 250 homes scheduled to be built. Currently, it is a set change in progress, a non space drifting until the appropriate permissions are gathered and signed.

The wicket laid waste in tilting wild grass, obliterating the

Freedom of information/request lingers long and then expires/ file as case closed

"I can't go on. I'll go on"

53.26234°N, 2.12894° W

A season in hell / The Illuminations

The autobiography and sex life of Andy Warhol

Brave New World

A Clockwork Orange

The Theatre and It's Double.

The Idiot

Nausea

Steppenwolf

Thus Spoke Zarathustra

Twilight of the Idols

Books in the personal library of Ian Curtis

Aspirational scholastic architecture / postcode affirmation of potential/ past life awaits bureaucrat's stamp /

Gain stops play

potential of play, memory site of leather on willow on flesh, fast disappearing into an estate agent's virtual walkthrough.

Satiated by the exemplary manifestation of the unforeseen metaphor underwriting our excursion we turn south and make our way to the terminal point of our reconnaissance.

"Please keep your distance

The trail leads to here"

Candidate (1979)

Hopes of a closure, of a denouement are dashed before we even gain entrance. "This location is protected by Alpha and Omega security", announces a board attached with zip lock to the flaking, blackened gates of the cemetery.

Our beginning is in our end, each staging post was only ever a fold in the fabric of time and space, there was no narrative to reconstruct as the journey unspooled. We were only ever tourists in messianic time with an off peak day return, non refundable, non transferable.

Curtis was cremated and on locating the small grey marker stone, one among many others, like the house on Barton Street that declined to consent to veneration, we are at once enthralled and appalled.

The ground around the discrete death notice resembles a collision between a shamanic votive altar and an outsider art clearing house. A savant curated assembly of coins, plectrums, cigarettes, ceramics, scrawled messages, fading photographs, desiccated flowers in cellophane wrap, and, perhaps most ominously a bound text authored by a recent pilgrim.

Fearing the worst, I open the document. It contains a sheaf of word-processed pages. The text is narrowly spaced, with optional punctuation and as the sheets flip past under my fingers, the white voids between the paragraphs dissolve leaving blocks of undifferentiated inscription.

I scan the screed looking for a clue to emerge, a justification for

Capital accretions /soul mortgage / time to downsize

Walking as evidence of unexpected confirmation/ hidden energy of change revealed through subtle encounters The afterlife has a bodyguard

53.26626°N,2.13717°W

Memorial security for the post biometric

Endings are (and can only be)

Beginnings

Let down by time/ expectations

Linger / deferred in the always

/already starting/started/ the mistake is thinking it starts

Pilgrim offering/layering in the

Endless accumulation /debris memorial / writing that must be read

Fever dream script / what was the author/ when will the reader

Begin to decipher/ and for what

the book's presence, for our presence here today. Why the book should be in my hands.

"I don't think there is an obstinacy more wrong than to believe in change, sometimes some things are sadly impossible"

Yes that's it. We've been looking for the past and all we seem to have located is change and the impossibility of return. We turned up forty years late to begin our inquiry. All the properties have altered. Locations have had their narrative imposed upon them from outside and elsewhere, a collective myth formed around an image. A set of circumstances that resist a satisfactory analysis. By undertaking an inquiry, the likelihood of authentic encounter recedes further out of reach.

Paying our last respects to the elusive ghost we walk away, back into life, off the trail.

"we've been moving round in different situations"

No Love Lost (1977)

Walking

The

Pharmakon

The first time I saw the word AstraZeneca was after taking a job in an investment firm on the outskirts of Edinburgh just after the turn of the millennium. I had no idea what an investment firm did but this did not seem to trouble the people at the interview, who reassured me that I would be trained and guided through the curious ways of the stock market.

This sounded fine. I was not long out of university and raised on an eighties pop culture diet of conspicuous consumption and newsreels of young men in stripy shirts and braces brandishing fistfuls of fifties whilst pouring champagne for adoring female entourages. Lacking the imagination for anything else I signed on for a tour of duty in late stage capitalism, inwardly perturbed at the reaction this might create with my more politically engaged friends and acquaintances.

My job was to go through a broker report each morning working out the values of the buys and sells from the previous day's trading. At the end there would be a net figure that needed to be transferred somewhere else. On completion of the task, the manager and I would go for lunch. In the afternoon we would answer the odd phone call and talk about football.

The manager was three years older than me and already had two flats and a convertible sports car. He had left private school at sixteen, dyslexic and with no qualifications. A family connection had got him a job in the post room and within two years he had a desk, a phone, and an attitude. He was cynical, prone to rage and generally hungover. Despite this he seemed to like me and appreciated my ability to correct the grievous linguistic violence of his emails before they sped away to our eminently respectable clients. I played a willing, somewhat confused pupil to his bleary eyed, crumpled mastery.

"Drugs."

I had asked him about a curious word that had appeared on the account one sunny, blue sky morning. The office we occupied looked out over the Pentland hills and the colours of spring were emerging. Clouds drifted across the steep slopes of the sheep speckled topography.

"They manufacture and sell drugs."

A small detail drew into focus amidst a mass of blurry uncertainty. AstraZeneca were a pharmaceutical company. I enjoyed looking at the word, the inclusion of the first and last letters of alphabet, the hint of stars and interplanetary conjunctions, the nod towards an eastern wisdom practice. It sounded modern and ancient, like a minor angel in a Blakean epic.

Someone had spent £60K the day before acquiring a piece of the company. I had slowly become accustomed to handling large transactions. Initially, the proliferation of zeros had terrified me. It was not until the master/manager advised "don't stress over anything under a million" that I was able to relax into the process of following the money and making sure it got to where it should.

A few desks down from me two nineteen year olds spent their days sorting through income statements. I was shocked and amused to hear one say to the other

"Don't worry about that £14 million, I've found it "

 His colleague nodded as if 50 p had been picked up off the floor.

04.08.22

This was a solo walk. I had no real idea of what I was trying to achieve with this one. I didn't want to apologise or explain. I had intention but lacked justification.

Circumnavigating the vast AstraZeneca site that lies on the outer northern edge of Macclesfield appeared to be possible. I had surveyed the site on google maps and while no actual pathways were discernible from the virtual drone view, there were no obvious obstacles either.

The campus employed about 4000 people and was made up of a patchwork of offices, industrial buildings, carparks, roads, and walkways. It bordered a residential area and was defined by the canal to the east and the dual carriageway to the west. I had made reconnaissance forays in the weeks prior and was struck by the soft border of the entry gate, the neatly kept flower gardens, surveillance cameras and the welcome signs that bid you stay away unless you were accredited.

I had set off at 10:30am on a warm morning. The forecast suggested rain would fall intermittently, but the temperature would remain high rising to the mid 20's by lunchtime. An uncommonly hot and reassuringly polarised English summers day.

10.30 GMT   AZN.L 10,732   open   London GBP   market cap 167.6B

Laurie Anderson, the performance artist, and musician had once taken a job at a McDonald's restaurant in New York as research for a show she was developing. Working unrecognised she said of the experience

"the people there, the workers were having a good time"

I couldn't help thinking her view was tinted by the always open option to return to the international art circuit when the happy meals started frowning back. None the less, as I began to plan the expedition, I began considering the tactic as a means to gain access to this town out with the town.

I opened up a recruitment website and searched.

Release manager - £500 per day would suit a "purposeful disruptor"

User experience designer - £70K – high level information architecture and low level flow   knowledge essential

Data Lake engineer - £60K – experience of lifecycle management and hypercare as a prerequisite

It felt like applying for a job as a footnote to an as yet unpublished Deleuze manuscript.

I was unqualified and lacking the language to consider a legitimate entry into the pharma citadel.

No option but to walk the lines of force around the forbidden city.

"Welcome to Macclesfield Campus

Turning Molecules in to Medicines "

11.30
AZN.L   10780p up
48

Campus (a. L. field)

The site is located in an area known as Hurdsfield

Medicines – Pharmakaon – the kill/cure – poison/remedy

speak/write

memory/erosion of memory

Walking to obtain the writing to create an understanding

Or

Writing of the walking to understand the creation

Or

Creative walking / writing toward understanding

I was able to enter so far along the outer perimeter, past a five a side football pitch and a multi storey carpark. Then the architecture began to repel any advance. Gated pathways, sentry boxes,

"authorised personnel only beyond this point"

I was at the borderline between civilian stroller and validated insider. Without the necessary papers I was forced to continue crablike, sidereal, mystified.

11.40 AZN.L 10788 p up8

The signposts steered me to the east, EXIT

A broad flat expanse of tarmac with white line grids

Sparsely occupied by a handful of cars

Post pandemic homework

In the corner a white van marked

SECURITY

There was something benign about its presence

I imagined that inside a mannequin sat

In grey guards' uniform with a flask of tea

Staring   wall eyed

At a monitor   with a time stamp

Contemplating my image

Unable   to move

Like a museum exhibit

Of a cold war situation room

Frozen out of time

Paint flaking from inanimate cheeks

The hands of the clock always and forever

at five minutes to twelve

I felt surveilled by hypnosis , telepathic redirection , mind tricks to alter the course.

I complied and drifted further along the periphery. I was being conducted offsite and the white noise traffic rush of the road on the border enveloped everything , a saturation of steel and hydrocarbon acoustics.

At the junction where the site concedes the territory to the town a gravel pathway opened up. It appeared to head north with a brown brick wall to the left and dense, varied vegetation to the right. Here was an interzone, where the unaccredited could walk the footprint of the forbidden municipality.

The sky was darkening to a thick woollen grey, as if the area suffered its own microclimate. I checked over my shoulder and back in the town proper a cloudless blue canopy hung still over the rooftops.

I trudged on, crunching the grit and stone of the path, soothed by traffic ambience. I began compiling a gazetteer of the undergrowth and the graffiti tags that animated either side of the narrow passage through which I walked.

ERROR   Cotoneaster

                                                                     Lathyrus

                                                                     Snowberry

A hollow oak would shield me from the wind   Oak

LEERO   Lime   Tilia

KASE

                                                          Rosa Scabrosa

JOOV
      Ghostberry

                                          Elderberry

                                          "cleanse the blood, clear the skin"

CRIME   Herb Robert

                                          "an herb of Venus, for all it hath a
                                          man's name"/   "effectual in
                                          old ulcers in the privy parts"

CI *Large bind-weed bells*   Bind weed

CR   Stinking Willie

                                          "I commend it for an universal

                                          medicine for the

                                          womb"

                                                          Phacelia

CRIME   *that shakes the elm trees mossy arms*   Elm "a cold

saturnine plant/

sovereign balm

for green wounds"

Sycamore

Rubus "I know no
great virtues in
the leaves"

Plantago "prevails
mightily against
tormenting pains"

SILO   Viburnum

The larks that in the thistle shield   Creeping Thistle

"the Greek   word Acanthus,
signifies any thistle whatsoever.

MARY Z

"BEWARE – Pedestrians, joggers and cyclists use this site"

11.50
AZN.L
10820p up
40

The wall to the left varied in height so the oncoming vehicles on the road below shifted in and out of view. The thick, green shield to the right occasionally broke down to reveal a metal fence topped with barbed wire. Glimpses of the interior were afforded by gaps in the foliage that entangled the mesh barrier.

Pipes, portacabins, plastic tubing, mirrored windows

Airconditioning vents, corroded paint, stone chip pathways

Not a solitary soul visible

Backstage boredom, no clues

I paused on the path to let a cyclist pass. Proving the warning of the sign. At my feet was a fast-food coffee cup.

Opposite to the entrance to the complex there was a McDonalds restaurant. Here, a mile down the road the waste footprint could be surveyed. A data point. I was starting to have fun.

11.55 AZN.L

10828p up 8

The Road Rumbled on Beside Me

The Silk Road, as it is known, carves a way out the town through the farm and footballer belt towards Stockport. Built in the 1990's it takes its name in deference to the textile manufacturing that propelled the town into modernity in the 18th and 19th century.

The local dignitaries liked to consider Macclesfield as the last outpost of the Silk Road trading route that had stretched for centuries from the Karakom mountains in southern China across Pakistan, the Hindu Kush , Afghanistan, Turkmenistan, Iran, the Levant, into the Mediterranean onto Italy and then arriving in England.

By 2011, The Silk Road had shifted meaning in the popular consciousness. It was the name employed by a virtual pharmacopoeia, a dark web trading platform specialising in the sale of high quality illegal narcotics. Shut down by the FBI in 2014, it was not until 2020 that investigators identified Bitcoin transactions linked to the site worth hundreds of millions of dollars.

that the historical unravelling

of the name should match

with such congruence

the embodied geography of the locale,

a multi billion dollar company

sells

pharmaceuticals, pharmakon, drug

on the silk road on

the right
side of the law.

1.57 AZN.L 10875p up 47

Reviewing the satellite map on my phone, I realised I had reached the sharp apex of the wedge of territory that the site occupied. It had started raining and I put on a bright orange cagoule. High viz, an act of sympathetic magic, attempting to summon up the workers who remained invisible on the other side of the treelined wire fence.

I came to a clearing dominated by the struts of an electricity pylon, a link in the power lines stretching out towards the horizon. Stinging nettles clustered round the metal feet.

Urtica Dioica

part of the anglo saxon

nine herbs charm

netelan / stune

the one who grows on stone/ grinds away pain

three pathways converge   here

        I pick the one to the right, I now have open countryside to my left,

ambient cattle ruminate silently.

As if from nowhere I am suddenly in the company of another. He is dressed in fluorescent yellow work wear, hunched in a chair his back towards me. He is facing a turnstile, as one might see at a football stadium or a prison. Designed to keep people out and in. He glances from the portal to me, scans me up and down for a second before returning his scrutiny to the revolving gate that will not turn for me. He read me right as persona non grata. Without papers or letters of introduction. Riff raff with a nil threat rating.

Hogweed

And then the canal is glanced through the trees. The north western passage is complete.

Hazel – "under the dominion of Mercury". *Corylus avellana* grows by the

stone bridge. /" very good to help an old cough"

 I am glad to cross water, a barrier that works for me, puts space between myself and the pull of the site. I feel safer, less at the will of the location more in control of the survey, the drift around the edges.

Hairy Willowherb, *Epilobium hirsutum*

or loosestrife / "often used in gargles for sore mouths, as also for the secret parts"

From the canal tow path, the location remains obscured by trees, however, I can see rooftops, chimneys and pipework. Mystery remains but I feel closer to a purpose. I am watching the site while it watches me, surveillance as a bi lateral asymmetrical exchange.

Whatever happens in there remains opaque, but it occurred for a short space of time in partnership with my walk.

The path is long narrow and straight. I've walked it before, back and forth. it does not hold any great enigma, I know my destination and can even visualise the point where the canal path reconnects with the road network.

The first half of the circumnavigation was uncertain, the discovery of the pathway along the Silk Road was unexpected, the second half is to walk in certitude.

Red clover – *Trifolium pratense*

          Hawthorn – *Crataegus monogyna* /a tree of Mars/good
for inward tormenting pains.

Walking/ breathing – counting the inhalation /exhalation

        One

                     Two

           a passing canal boat

the thread is lost   so begin
again

             inflate/deflate

One

      two

              three

   a heron

      still amongst the reeds

 hold my breath

             remaining at
zero

           12.09 AZN.L 10853p
up19

Rumex Crispus /curled dock /   "cleanses the blood, and strengthens the
liver."

Artemisia vulgaris /mugwort/"to help the delivery of the birth, and expel the after-birth"

Heracleum / hogweed

"never less alone than when alone"   Browne

meandering on

the heron's wings beat the skin of the air

walking/breathing

forgetting to

count

Butterbur – "exceeding good in violent and pestilential fevers "

Petasites / from the family Asteraceae

- lacking a ZN but it will do

I can hear men at work on the other side of the canal beyond the tree lined fence, shouts, clanks of metal on metal, on stone. The insistent bleeps of reversing loaders. A radio plays pop music. The sounds recede into the stillness of the summer heat and my feet pad and grate in regular cadence on the dry, loose earth of the path.

Sipping water from my bottle, I look up to see the cloud towers piled high in the wide sky, white columns, bulbous and ragged edged, ranging across the deep blue expanse.

The walk has achieved its intention, a circumnavigation, a tour of the corporate edifice, but I feel no closer to the interior. The act of the walk has perhaps inscribed a meaning into the landscape, a possibility of interaction , a shared passage.

Crossing the canal at a neatly curved bridge, I re-enter the undergrowth, the overgrowth of the perimeter. I can hear the traffic that circulates incessantly around the pharma complex. Delivering, removing, people, equipment, product in endless circulation.

I make one last approach to the perimeter fence, the view resolutely obscured in thick greenery. As I edge my way along I tread upon an object in the tangles of grass and wildflowers. Reaching down I flip over the stumbling block. It's a plastic road sign marooned from its site of significance,

ROAD

CLOSED

White capitals against a fresh blood red background. The surface had been detourned in black spray paint. No words emerge from the coiling aerosol script. A thread of erasure, a retaliation, of wilful opposition. Double negation of the road. Possibilities cancelled, the journey culminates in a sign out of context and illegible.

12.17 AZN.L 10889 up36

Later that evening back at home, I arrive at some kind of evidence of collaboration between my walk and the site. I'd recorded the walk on a GPS phone app. I can see the time elapsed, the distance covered, the elevation gained. A quantitative experience, the walk as data, calibrated, stored on a cloud server, awaiting exploitation, a monetised afterlife as a push notification, a timeline advert.

I search for news items on AstraZeneca, and quickly touch my way to the share price movement for the day. The correspondence I was seeking throughout the day reveals itself as I examine the price data. At 10am the stock is in a trough around the 10700 mark, by 1030, when I left the house, AZN.L starts a steep ascent to 10720 and continues to rise steadily throughout the morning. By midday it has edged higher to 10850, maintained an upward trajectory and then plateaued as my walk drew to a close.

My walk had been clockwise, and I begin wondering if this added centrifugal movement of the environment around the periphery had in some way agitated the trading activity on the exchanges. I feel duped, an unwilling corporate shill, boosting the imaginary value, speeding up the flow of untaxed, untraced dividends to offshore banking centres.

I resolve to return at a later date and make a counterclockwise survey. A speculative widdershins wander to reverse any capital gains.

walking/reading/

writing/memory

1793/1983/2022

Growing up I had two accents. At home I spoke as someone from the western central belt of Scotland speaks, reflecting the annunciation, emphases, and tones of both my parents. This was not something that I was really even aware of until I went to school and was surrounded by people who spoke Estuary English. This led to my own appropriation of the sounds uttered by people who live in Surrey, the county in which I was born and lived. I was able to cast off this makeshift accent when I returned home each day and reapply it when I entered the school gates reluctantly the next morning. I don't recall if I was being taught to speak with an English accent or if it just occurred by immersion. Either way it happened, and it stuck.

By the age of seven or eight my vowel speaking voice was flexible depending on my environment. The transition between the two modes was unconscious and I don't recall it presenting problems. My domestic life and my external life were fairly separated experiences so the change in registers passed generally unnoticed from day to day.

This all changed when I was nine years old, and my family returned to live Scotland. Suddenly I was living in a world where the inside and the outside all spoke in the same way. My exterior accent put me at odds with my classmates. I was different.

A period of modification occurred. I learned to maintain the sound of my voice in all circumstances. By the time I reached secondary school the realignment was complete, I could pass for Scottish. Occasionally, my geographic origins would betray me and I would slip back, uttering "suh ink" rather than "something". Ears would prick up and some schoolboy remonstrations would occur.

My parents moved the family to Ayr, about an hour away from their own hometown of Motherwell, on the west coast of the country around 40 miles southwest of Glasgow. On arrival at school, I was quickly introduced to the study of the works of Robert Burns.

Burns was, and still is, a big deal in Ayr. He was born and educated there and started his literary career from the town. Scanning through the biographies it's clear that he also left the town fairly early on and Dumfries appears to have as much a claim on his poetic endeavours as any other place.

The reading and reciting of Burns was a requisite part of the education system in the area. It was also competitive, and each year Burns speaking competitions proliferated. School and civic pride was very much at stake in these events.

My first encounter with his work stayed with me. The class was given handouts with the poem "Willie's Wife". We were instructed to copy the poem out into our books or "jotters" as they were referred to by the teacher. It was here that I started to experience difficulties.

The first lines read

"Willie Wastle dwalt on Tweed

The spot they ca'd it Linkumdodie.

Willie was a wabster guid

Could stown a clou wi ony body"

The poem was written in hybrid Scots in the late 18th century. Nearly 200 years later I needed a translation to get at the meaning.

Roughly it reads – William Wastle lived by the River Tweed at a location known as Linkumdodie. William was a skilled weaver and could pack a ball of thread as well as anyone.

At the time I knew that I liked the sounds but had no idea as to their meaning or context. Intrigued and confused I persevered and began to understand.

By the second year of high school Burns was featuring high in the curriculum and it was at this point that we were presented with Tam O Shanter, generally regarded as the poet's masterpiece. What struck me most acutely was that the drama unfolds in a recognisable location with clearly defined landmarks and placenames. I lived a mile or so from Brig a Doon and the Auld Kirk and regularly walked the environment described in the poem. I was inhabiting a literary imagining of place. The meeting of geographical reality with aesthetic production felt valuable though I did not yet have the critical tools to begin developing the idea.

Fast forward 35 years and I attempt to write a translation of Tam O Shanter, the one my teenage self needed to understand what was going on. I chose to remove all the English words leaving the Scots phrases intact and in their original place in the text, The next move was to replace them with the corresponding English terms and allow the poem to compose itself anew, letting the white spaces on the page assemble without intervention.

An advance and a retreat, a linguistic decolonisation followed by a postcolonial reassertion of meaning. It's an attempt to speak about the complexity of historical associations and the difficulty of beginning again when the world has changed inexorably from the initial contact between cultures.

By withdrawing the English terms from the text, the Scots words hang together with a raw inscrutability, they have become unknowable to the people whose inheritance they represent.

Back in the classroom, all the pupils needed a translation of the poem. The meaning as it had been constructed in 1793 was inaccessible two centuries later. The Scots language had faded from the common language, it was a trace of something that had become stranded in an entangled and contentious history. Although It was present and loaded with significance it was also absent, ghostly and indistinct. A call across time seeking a receiver.

Tom Of

      street dealers
    dry neighbours, neighbours

And   take
       boozing   strong ale,
       replete   uncannily
       not   long
            gaps
                home,

found   *Tom*
   from   one
(Old   that never
         pretty girls.)

  Tom!   so
   taken   own
    told   well   rascal,
  loquacious   babbler;
    from
Each   not

   every quantity of corn, with
     long   silver;
    horse   driven
      got   drunk

caught with   darkness,
        old   church.

                    makes   cry,
            many
      many
        from

              That
Tom   located oddly profoundly;
      hearth, blazing
with overrunning cups,
              Shoemaker
              thirsty
Tom loved   true brother;
            pissed   together.
      drove   with tales   gossip;
    as
              Tom
With
    cobbler told

roar
Tom   not

so
Even   himself amongst glasses:
      fly home with loads

with

    all

fly

No
            Tom must
                                    stone,

     such   takes

it would blow

            long,

     Devil

Well

Tom thrashed   puddle and swamp,

                    good
                    old
                    with
     spectres
Church
Where ghosts   owls

Where,   snow, the dealer choked;
          birch tree   huge stone,

Where   broke his neck
          gorse,   grave,
Where   found   child;
          hawthorn, above
Where   mother   herself

Church   blaze;
      every hole

With weak beer,   no
With whisky
      drinks so frothed   *Tommie*'s brain,
            cared for devils not a bit
                  greatly

upon my soul *Tom*   uncanny

No   brought   from

   window seat
         old Devil
      tangled ruffian
      give
         assembled   made   scream,

all   vibrated
               box bed
showed
          incantation
   cold

Tom
              holy
              bones   irons;
Two handspans long small,   children;
            from   rope,
With   mouth
           with blood
           with

              own

handle;

With   fastening   cloth;

                       corner.

     Tommie

seize,
     every witch sweated   stank,
     cast off   clothing   work,
vigourous   blouse!

Tom,   Tom!   teenage girls,
All
        slips,   greasy flannel,
        snow   hundred linen!
These trousers

          once   good
     would have given   buttocks,
          one glimpse of the pretty girls!

old   half crazed
gnarled   would wean
Leaping   twisted horn,
          didn't

Tom knew   all elegant,
                              beautiful,

(Long   known
   many
        many handsome
                 both large

     short chemise, of   coarse linen
          girl

                         jaunty.—
      knew
   blouse   purchased   little
With two pounds   (it was all

must hide;
Such
                    folded and flung,
   supple harlot   strong),
     Tom   one
                 eye
                    restlessly content,
   hopped   strength:
        one frolic, next another,
Tom lost   all together

       'Well   short skirt'

buzz with   itch
                  nest
    louse

With many

Tom! *Tom*!   away!
              heron!
              coming!
        woeful

   stone   bridge;

      stone
  fiend

        pressed
         intention
     knowledge
One   pull,
       own
   witch siezed

whoever
each

short night dress
                over
    Tom

The poem and the location of the poem can be walked in various ways. For myself, the landscape is a familiar one, I can traverse it as a convenient way home, a piece of literary imagination, an opportunity to survey the ruins of a 15th century church, a reminiscence of teenage wanderings, a meditation on the marketing strategy of the Ayrshire tourist board.

I need not be present in the location to experience these alternate readings, I have place as memory, as recall. Something that can be played forward and back, frozen and zoomed in on. The location, and the movement through the location is embodied, it is part of me.

The walking that occurred as a child, a teenager, adult, accumulated into a sediment of experience and knowledge, enabling a variety of interpretations all of them valid and intertwined.

The poem of Tam o Shanter can be navigated in a similar fashion. It operates as psychosexual drama, a deliberation on the omnipresence of the church in 18th century Scotland, a morality tale on temperance, an occult dabbling. All working simultaneously and to be employed or disregarded as the readers sees fit.

Through schooling and geographical coincidence, parts of the poem are stuck in my head, I can't forget them, the rhythms are fixed, phrases indelibly inscribed. Over time the language of the place and the place itself are similarly embodied. Walking and reading into a meaning that is felt and thought, a nostalgia and a possibility.

ASTREA

0

Being a walk in fifteen parts.

Mary Fitton resurrects with a dark demeanour – The church at Gawsworth – "affection is false" Mary is a language subject – the walk commences – origins in a dream – the walk continues – enter the fool – Mary and the fool converse – we arrive at the church – some thoughts on walking with others – the colonial landscape – Mary despondent and then consoled – traces of the war machine – and in summary – exit (into the pastoral)

1

stillness	chapel	marble	mottled
glows	soft	candle	light
wick	human	hand	lit
black	black	pitch	night
without	sound	centuries	magnifies
the	slightest	the	lesser
until	sleep	dream	fades

soul	clap	emerging	figure

drifts   limned   tallow   glow

head   bowed   hands   prayer

up   over   hover   sepulchre

hanging   wingless   angel   weeping

descends   stone   flags   chapel

black   black   cannot   fathomed

definition   lost   tenebrous   hollows

dark   lady   unseen   midnight

passes   bolts   oak   door

graveyard   pausing   remember   names

centuries   elapsed   modify   time

sped   sky   blur   rush

moon   fine   crescent   drop

east   horizon   mist   morning

air   seamless   earth   sky

dark   lady   stands   pool

causes   time   return   joint

wood   pigeon   morning   note

herself   reflected   beneath   tower

unattended   makes   watery   mirror

face   mystery   blackened   shroud

cerecloth   ink   blot   black

cast cloak velvet deep

silk trim ebony brocade

hands gloved blackened calfskin

weightless dusk black boots

fine laced darkest thread

touching air above ground

she floats   turns

times fast ice others

slow summer leaf encounter

twist smoke glint pearl

twigs crack underfoot forest

sleek black cat repeated

summon up day spirits

assemble turn bow curtsey

  origin disposition

pleased servile politics court

spins three pivot air

  touches ground

alder wand taps air

crack stone thrown glass

shocks morning mists echo

"fair counted not was black age old the in"

                              The scene swells and shimmers,
                              heads keening to her voice

"name beauty not bore it were it if or"

                    The gargoyles on the chapel doorways animate
              their eyes flit here and there

"heir successive beauty's black now is but"

                              The sleek black cat unfurls wings that
                    beat womp womp on the   air

"shame bastard a with slandered beauty and"

              At this a servant, in fine cloth tunic, shrivels to a stick
              thin man and dissolves to dust

"power nature's on put hath hand each since for"

                              The sliver of moon tilts and drips blood into

                    the clouds that swiftly formed a chalice to collect

"face borrowed false art's with foul the fairing"

                    The dark lady rises higher to the
              clocktower throws her arms wide

"bower holy no name no hath beauty sweet"

                    Her voice shivers the branches of the cedar tree
              that hangs over the assembly

"disgrace in lives not if, profaned is but"

                              She swoops as the hawk strikes
                    the mouse in the field

"black raven are eyes, mistress' my therefore"

                              The air turn to ice /all is
frozen

all is still

She floats amongst her court

peers deep into the eyes

and frozen soul

of her maid

The dark lady makes herself

small as pin prick and alights

upon her servant's nose.

Her voice redounds as if the
mountains, stars and sky   are at
war

She reappears

at size and scale

the entourage breathes

the freeze released

her head revolves right round and
round and round again

her eyes examine each and every soul present

content that the work has begun she lets the daybreak

a cockerel cries the light returned and dew blooms on the grass tufts
underfoot.

clouds turned pink from moonblood drips

are now sped away offstage and the blue of dawn

envelops the world that is so dark has been so dark

then shoos her court to the

graves and the hollows

and struts the earth in solitude

2

Nickolaus Pevsner, in his exhaustive guide to the architecture of Cheshire, describes St James in Gawsworth as "a very strange church". Festooned with hunky punks and water draining gargoyles, it has sat in an idyllic locale since the late 15th Century.

Were it only for its age, beauty, and architectural idiosyncrasies (it has no aisles) it would have remained an off the beaten track exemplar of a forgotten version of England. A blue rinse, tory cream tea hallucination of a world that never actually did exist.

It is the additional historical scintilla of the presence of Mary Fitton in the funerary tombs in the rear of the chapel that generates an extra time shifting, century traversing, intrigue. Mary was a lady in waiting to Elizabeth I, and had this been her only claim on immortality it would have put her in the first league of local historical luminaries. Her memory is given an additional twist by the possibility that she is the Dark Lady of Shakespeare's sonnets. George Bernard Shaw had her as a likely candidate and it was not until the 1920's that she was taken out of the running following the discovery of a portrait depicting her with an alabaster white complexion.

3

"In June 1600 Mary led a dance in the masque celebrating the fashionable wedding of Lady Anne Russell, granddaughter of the Earl of Bedford, with Henry Somerset, later created Marquess of Worcester, at Lord Cobham's residence in Blackfriars. Led by Mary, the maids performed an allegorical dance and afterwards chose substitutes from the audience. Mary boldly chose the queen, telling her that she represented Affection (which then meant passionate love), to which the queen replied "Affection? Affection's false"."

Michael Brennan, Noel Kinnamon, Margaret Hannay, *Letters of Rowland Whyte to Sir Robert Sidney* (Philadelphia, 2013), p. 501

4

03.08.22

"J and I leave the house with the dog in tow, each of us moving slowly in a heat seared mid morning shuffle. We plod along the busy A536 single file. The traffic is too loud to have a conversation and it moves so fast that anything beyond a solemn trudge seems an unnecessary risk with the slipstream of passing juggernauts wobbling the stride. We keep our heads down and continue until the opportunity to break free of the incessant roar and rush occurs at the periphery of Gawsworth village."

5

"E blanc"

Back in June he had woken up one morning with the word "Astrea" fixed in his mind. This dream vestige was stripped of its context, no melting images in his mind's eye to accompany the outcropping from his subconscious. He ran through possible interpretations. Could it be justice, the 8th Tarot card? Consulting AE Waite He discovered a reading - "equity, rightness, triumph of the deserving side of law" – none of which resonated. He then fell back into considering Frances Yates and her essay "Queen Elizabeth as Astraea" where she argues that the term had been a Spenserian symbol for Elizabeth I. This felt more in sync.

He had recently become interested in the chapel at the nearby village of Gawsworth the ancestral family home of the Fitton family. The daughter of the house had historically documented links to the Elizabethan court. He'd been deferring a visit to the location for a while, so as the weather was good he got on his bike and cycled the three miles to verify if this dream word was the beginning or the end of something.

Arriving at the church yard at 10am, he dismounted and lent his bike against a bench. He walked amongst the gravestones to the path that led to a solid door. A circular iron handle hung from the weathered oak panels. He grasped it gently, turning it slowly.

The latch lifted and he entered the deserted church. Hymn books lay in neat piles by a large stone font. On either side of the central passage the pews stood empty. The air retained a scent of flowers fading and dust motes circulated in the morning sun.

He walked to the chancel screen and picked out the Fitton family monument in the gloom of the far corner of the chapel. It was a pious family grouping, the wife and the children carved in life size marble, solemnly standing by the tomb of the departed father. He recognised Mary Fitton from the photographs in local history books. She was partially obscured by the contrite figure ahead of her in the composition, her face a mystery.

He turned from the tomb and glanced up towards the stained-glass windows that lined each side of the church. Amongst the saints and the stations of the cross his eye fell upon the image of bird, wings spread beneath a regal crown against a blue background. Encircled by a white border it was inscribed within "per ardva ad astra", the e missing, a blank, an aporia, withheld in the dream.

6

"We walk through the village, expanded now with housing developments from the 30's, 50's,80's, the present. Stopping at the community shop for water and coffee, we take in the shop widow display. Large A4 print letters "50% off". Amongst the signage are images of the queen from various points in her reign. The unintentional collage floating the idea of the firm trading at a deep discount, the stock that tanked on courtroom controversy and boardroom departures. In the garden next door, a union flag hangs lank, occasionally fluttering in the warm breeze."

7

A quarter mile down the road from the chapel lies the grave marker for another local celebrity. Samuel "Maggoty" Johnson is generally regarded as the last professional jester in England. He maintained a side hustle as a playwright and his eccentric work "Hurlothrumbo" played for 7 weeks on the London stage in 1729. Employing the alias Lord Flame, he relocated to Cheshire and lived on as the fool and dancing master to the family at the nearby Gawsworth Hall. He lived on until 1773 dying aged 82. His tomb nestles in a patch of hilly woodland inscribed "Stay thou to whom chance directs or eye persuades, to seek the quiet of the sylvan shades."

8

disturbances at the graveyard

run through the undercommons to

the grave of the fool

with no choice

but to perform, he rises

shakes off 250 years of sleep

and shuffles with bells trembling

towards the end of the lane, to the sight of

the dark lady muttering at nothing

he approaches

attempts to "cool a courtesan"

she is raving now, that she had been libelled in the history books

marked as the mistress of a mystery

the strange news had flown up and down the astral pathways

circulating in the gossip of the spectral ancestry

until it dropped into her sleeping ear that lived

on within the marble that enclosed her for 400 years

she glares at the fool

who glares back

as a mirror they each the other match

the fool speaks

"this cold night will turn us all to fools and madmen"

"my thoughts and my discourse are as madmen's are" she utters

"yes indeed: thou wouds't make a good fool" he replies

"mad slanderers by mad ears believed be" she wails

"when slanders do not live in tongues/ then shall the realm of Albion

come to great confusion" he counsels

"how can I put fair truth upon so foul a face" she asks

"truths a dog must to kennel" he offers

"what of "the breath that from my mistress reeks"" she quotes

"tis like the breath of an unfee'd lawyer" he quips

"that thy unkindness lays upon my heart" she sobs

"when a wise man gives thee better counsel, give me mine again" says
the fool and departs

9

*"We arrive at the churchyard, which is empty. J takes the dog on a walk
through the tombstones, and I/he rework(s) my/his initial visit from a couple
of months earlier. Once again I/he am/is the solitary inhabitant, the light
streams in through the stained glass, the Fitton family monument remains
static in the corner behind the altar. I/he wander(s) up and down the
passages dowsing for some new energy, a variant heat to absorb, but nothing
is offered. I/he leave(s) no further advanced, without a question, lacking an
answer."*

10

Walking with another offers the possibility of the unforeseen, the contingent, to assume centre stage. The other's alternative viewpoints, histories, sensory perceptions, tilt the narrative into the unexpected, disturbing the thought structures and habits that frame the solo walker's meditations. The other is also a witness, a guarantor, a validator. Walking as a shared encounter modifies the process of walking, it subverts the map, however loosely it was plotted out in advance.

11

"Closing the heavy oak door carefully behind me I blink into the sunlight and see J and the dog working their way back through the tombstones along the carefully swept path. J recalls that as a child she would attend outdoor theatre productions in the grounds of the Elizabethan Hall that stands behind the chapel. Picnics and deckchairs in the early evening summer sun set out in front of the stage. Often Shakespeare would be performed.

We continue our walk out past the churchyard and pass the entrance of the driveway that leads to the hall where the Fitton family resided. We are too early to pay a visit, the sign by the gate indicates the house is open from 2pm in the month of August. Admission £10.

J wants to walk further along the curving road, and we are soon alongside a row of cottages that back onto a courtyard and stables. Opposite there is an unexpected presence, another reminder from history, cast in bronze, silent yet full of tales.

12

The dark lady wails

Sending the crows to calling

Amidst the gloom of the trees

She turns herself invisible

And floats through the graveyard

Through the heavy rough stone

Of the boundary wall and into

The gardens of the hall that

Had been her home four centuries before.

She passes though the door as

Sand through hands slips softly

And drifts up the staircase

To the library where she surveys

The leather-bound tomes

Some as old as she some older

Her eye alights on the Shakespeare folio

And she shudders

At the slight that history has left her bearing

Further along the waxed wood shelf

She sees a newer book

That pricks upon her intuition

Turning it over in her glassy hands

She takes in the title

"The Genius of Shakespeare" by Jonathan Bate.

She skims across the pages and settles on a chapter

That promises to resolve the issue of ignominious identity

She is relieved to read that she is multitudes

Emilia Lanier, Lucy Baynham, Lucy Morgan,

The wife of John Florio, Jacqueline Field, Jennet Devanant

Among others among none

She closes the book, melts through the walls of the hall and

Before returning to the stone sleep of the centuries

Telepaths a message to the fool who has recomposed in eternity

In his grave a long the lane.

"I hate from hate away she threw

And saved my life saying –"not you"."

Above the fool's tomb a flame flickers in reception

And then out.

13

"We wind our way back along the lane towards the graveyard. I decide to make one last rotation around the church, hoping to draw down something unexpected from the gothic grotesquery of the chimeric carvings that jut from the parapets. On completing the circuit, I spy J sitting with the dog on a stone bench looking out to the lake that divides the site from the quiet road.

They rise as I rejoin them and reveal a memorial script incised into the buff grey rock of the seat. The text commends the reader to remember Denis Ziani de Ferranti who lived in the hall from 1937 to 1962. Denis was a scion of an engineering dynasty that diversified into lucrative associations with the military and weapons manufacturers only to collapse into bankruptcy when an investigation into illegal arms sales revealed the firm had drifted too deep in a deeply opaque world.

14

A walk through place can be a decoding. An attempt to discern an obscured narrative of location, a persistence of circumstance modulated over time, always returning to an original impetus, a helix of proliferation, an index of similitude.

At Gawsworth there is the origin story of the aristocrat, who is briefly transplanted to the Elizabethan court, the crucible of intent that devised the colonial project through maritime explorations, land grabs and the expansion of trade that translated people, place, and nature into capital. A speculation where the bets came up and the acquisitive leverage of dominion reshaped the territory, drew up a map where none had been, named and took away names.

From there the colonial initiative is transferred onto the symbol of the politician, the statesman who assumed power as an accessory to a privilege that had been born out of the exploitation of the earth and the living things of the earth. Preserved in bronze, left to stand in an out of the way corner of the English countryside.

Then the echoes of the military industrial complex, the workshop of the war machine, camouflaged in Tudor architecture and the postcard simulacra of the Christian pastoral daydream.

The genealogy of an ideology inscribed in the landscape, mutating in response to the times, avoiding scrutiny, keeping up the disappearances.

15

"J, the dog and I take the long way back through stubbled fields, passing oak trees settled in isolation, beneath the starflower blue sky."

Notes

"I watched it slip away"

The title, all song lyric quotations and details of the Ian Curtis library are taken from, So This Is Permanence, Joy Division Lyrics and Notebooks by Ian Curtis, edited by Deborah Curtis and Jon Savage; Faber and Faber, 2014.

Walking in the Pharmakon

The text includes quotations from The English Physitian by Nicholas Culpeper, 1652 and also lines from the poems of John Clare.

Stock market price data obtained the iPhone Stocks app.

walking/reading/writing/memory/1793/1983/2022

The translation was made using The Dictionary of the Scots Language www.dsl.ac.uk

Astrea

The speech of Mary Fitton is assembled from quotations from the Sonnets (127-152)

The speech of the fool/Lord Flame/Samuel "Maggoty" Johnson is assembled from the Fool's part in King Lear.

Aspects of this text were influenced by the plenary session "Walks through Colonial Britain" delivered by Corrine Fowler, Raj Pal and Emily Zobel Marshall at the English Shared Futures Conference, Manchester, July 8th, 2022.

The work also exists as a physical object.

Scroll

Paper, ink, pencil, wood, felt, metal. 38cm x 12800cm (2022)

Always already in the both and

a statement of poetics

"Because it has always already begun, representation therefore has no end"

Jacques Derrida

"The background of this unusual book is not the European 'either-or', but a magnificently affirmative ' both-and '"

 Carl Jung

Place/Movement/Writing

"Walking is to lack a place" (Certeau,1984, p 103) affirms Michel Certeau and it is this suspension of location that I am interested in exploring, how the movement through place displaces the fixity of an environment and affords the opportunity, while the movement is in progress, to re-examine, rethink and rewrite place.

Karen Barad describes writing "which is neither fully discontinuous with continuity or even fully continuous with discontinuity, and in any case, surely not one with itself" (Barad, 2010, p 244) By embracing prose, poetry, quotation, data, chronologies, histories, fictions, and realisms I hope to generate a writing that is always becoming, that occurs on a plane of immanence, that is a plane of immanence.

My approach is to combine these two propositions/provocations in a series of four texts that seek to define place through movement.

I am attempting to inhabit what Ben Spatz refers to as a blue sky body "The body in its enfolded relations, where ecology is a process of both world making and world tending" Spatz (2020 p xv). This undertaking is at once active and ethical, it acknowledges the creative impulse must be aligned with an empathetic rigour and that the sense of being alive within a matrix of shared energy is a privilege and a responsibility. The active choices and ways of being within this context shape the future potentialities as they occur, making as we tend, tending as we make.

The texts deal with the act of walking and for this I am propelled forward by Nietzsche when he declares in aphorism 34 in the Twilight of the Idols "Only those thoughts that come by walking have any value". All of the journeys described occurred on foot, alone or with others and any insights or knowledge revealed or gained came through the process of walking or a reflection/diffraction after the event of the walk.

When I refer to place, I am led by the idea of Edward Casey that "places gather" (Casey 1996, p24) My reading of this is that the idea of place is always relational to and within and without the elements that constitute it. Place becomes a constellation of topography, history, habits, architecture, interpretations, imaginings. A place as an affinity, a gravity, an assembly of possibilities.

Autofiction /Autotheory/ location of the self

Mary Worthington describes autofiction as works that "constantly play with readerly expectations about memoir and fiction, thwarting both and thereby forcing a recognition that . . . the line is at times rather permeable" (Clare 2020, p85)

That all the texts are in part memoir but enhanced to a greater or lesser extent by fictions is central to the writing. The borderline between what did and did not happen and the inclusion and exclusion of events is one of the fundamental strategies in play in the writing. The text is in some sense a game, a puzzle, a joke. This in itself is all very well but leaves the reader (and the writer) in hall of mirrors uncertain whether they should laugh along or lean in toward the narratives. Autofiction mutes the emotional potential of a text.

An alternative approach is autotheory that attempts "to self-consciously and practically construct an ethical or sincere self in a critical manner". (Clare, 2020, p86). In my own writing I am working to follow this method, but the work is always only ever work in progress.

The texts are the writing of the self or variant of the self, or some other self playing the self, or a version of the self that fits the scenario, or a hybrid of selves that are continually reforming, dissolving into the becoming selfless.

How much is true or false depends on how much you/I want it to be true or false

Or can you/I rather move in the ambiguity

In the deferral of the definitive

So that the missing parts are ways in and out / to be filled in

Or left blank

To be a reliable disorientator

The work

In *"I watched it slip away"* I am interested in tensions. The text is arranged such that two modes of writing are working with and also in opposition to each other. They comment upon, affirm, and contradict one another, simultaneously pushing towards and away from a consensus of meaning.

The walk recorded in the text takes place with another, a significant extraneous variable that sends the narrative into unforeseen territories. The experience of the walk is continually at risk of destabilisation, however, this hazard in turn provides for unexpected developments and allows the experience and the document of the experience to move beyond authorly preconceptions.

The text as much as the walk becomes a collaboration between individuals, the presence or absence of significance is derived through mutual negotiation of the landscape and the knowledge, both covert and revealed, that it offers.

For *"Walking in the Pharmakon"* I am concerned less with idea of an ecopoetics and more with radical landscape poetics. This idea is foregrounded by Harriet Tarlo, who associates it with work that, "clings to its hold on the local and physical world; it is "from here"." (Tarlo, 2011. Page 7).

My intention was to employ a multiplicity of registers, voices, quotations inputs and memories to generate a writing that attempts to evoke and at the same time deconstruct ideas of place as well as the ideas that place brings into being.

The temporal experience of the walk is significant in this text. The activity occurs in a series of entangled and simultaneous vectors, the weather, the stock market, the seasonal variation of the plants are all at play and preclude the possibility of fixed meaning.

In *walking/reading/writing/memory/1793/1983/2022*, I am synthesising ideas of memoir, Oulipian constraint, translation, and postcolonial reflection into a hybrid of auto theoretical / poetocritical approaches. The poem is attempting to say what I could not write. The writing is attempting to say what the poem omits.

With regard to the translation, I am drawn to the possibilities of interpretation that the act of translation offers. Despite the rigid constraint that the text is defined by, individual word choice remains an entirely personal activity. The option to move the translation in and out of formal grammatical constructions and coherent causal relationships enables the writer to achieve a sense of asymmetrical co authorship.

As to the inclusion of personal memoir, it is striking that as one writes in this mode, one is constantly acknowledging both the passage of time and the impossibility of adequately articulating the difference between the writer and the subject (who are of course one and the same). This blind spot, or epistemic aporia haunts any attempt to write the self.

The text is not concerned with the political histories or future state of the relationship between Scotland and England. It is however wholly concerned with the irreversible language contacts that occurred between the two nations.

In *Astrea* I am looking at what Jenn Ashworth has described as apophenia, "the pathologically apophenic mind will imbue just about anything with meaning" (Ashworth,2019, p161.) It is a fiction within a real experience, the place in which the text unfolds is alive with interpretations, speculation, real and imagined narratives. The text works to draw together the historical fact and the historical error, the place as lived and imagined, the surface composition of changeless locale and the darker historical engines that shape the latent meanings and lines of force continually reconstituting readings of the location.

In this text, the collaborators on the walk operate as a counterbalance to the narrators apophenia. For them, a chair is just a chair, a church always and only a church. The walk is a shared but mutually exclusive experience, external realities mediated through differing interiors. The atmosphere of the encounter is modified by those present. On cannot step out on the same walk twice.

The Scroll

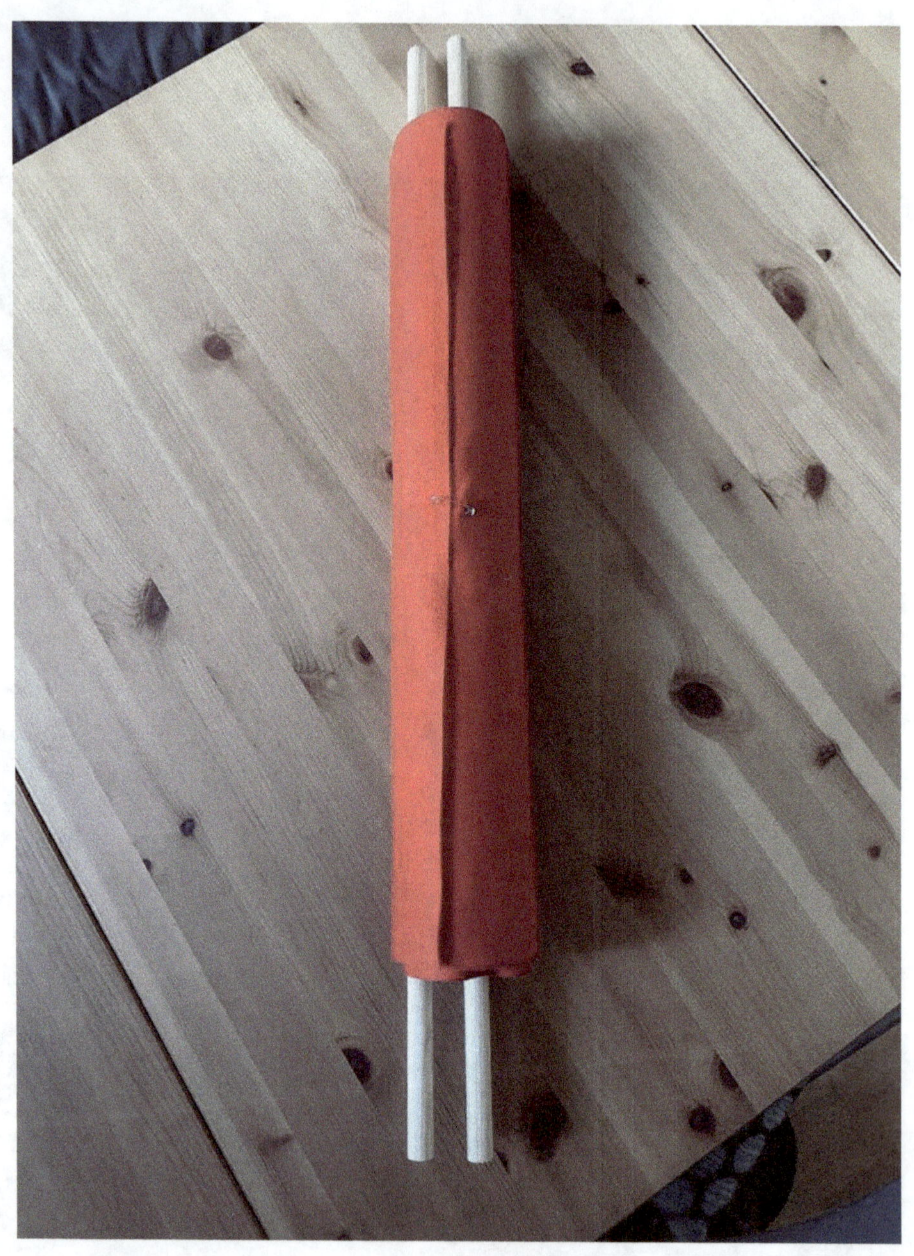

Scroll   2022
paper ink pencil wood felt metal
38 cm × 12800 cm

Before the book, before the codex, there was the scroll. Knowledge, narrative and information was recorded on long rolls of papyrus or animal skin. The handles at either end of the document allowed the reader to move through the text and the work could be safely and compactly stored when the reading was complete.

The idea to transfer my own text to a scroll came late in the process of composition. I was content with the editing and drafting of the work and was looking at ways to extend the possibilities of interpretation of the work by manifesting it as a physical object.

The scroll felt appropriate for several reasons.

1. As the work was about the process of walking, the mechanics and the manipulation of the scroll lent themselves well to idea of movement and echoed the way that a walk unfolds as a process of revealing through kinetic engagement.
2. I was taken by the idea that traditional East Asian scrolls, originating in the 7th century BCE, were considered to be a depiction of continuous narrative or journey. It suggested an early form of documentary, a cinematic exposition of experience.
3. That the scroll could be unfurled to its full length allowed for a survey of the text/journey as an entirety. In the same way that one might survey the valley and the mountain range from a peak reached after several hours or days of walking.

As I began work on the scroll the embodied nature of the process became apparent. After the first hour my hand ached and progress was slow. By the end of the first day, I had only a thousand words to show for my efforts. The following day progress improved, and I was surprised to find I had accumulated several thousand words by the time I stopped working. On day three I began to experience the process as calming and meditative, involving periods that could be described as a flow state, where time was experienced without pressure and decisions regarding textual arrangement were made quickly and without difficulty. By the fourth and final day I was spending periods of time looking at the scroll in various stages of unfurling and enjoying the experience of writing by hand, the sound of the pen scratching the surface, the smoothness of the paper against my skin and the soft brushing sensations of the object as it wound and unwound on the wooden tabletop.

My ideal sympathetic reader is encouraged to manipulate the scroll in all the ways that its construction allows for. Perhaps unfurl the scroll to its full length and walk around it, next to it, even upon it. Engage with the movement of the text as the handles revolve. Take time to examine lengths of the scroll and experiment with the opportunity that the spatial extension affords for transversal reading across sections of text. Allowing the eye, the body, and the mind to cohere in the process of reading as they did in the process of writing.

Bibliography

Jenn Ashworth, *Notes Made While Falling* (Goldsmiths Press, 2019)

Karen Barad, *Quantum Entanglements and Hauntological Relations of Inheritance*, Derrida Today, 2010, Vol. 3, No. 2, Special Issue: Deconstruction and Science (2010), pp. 240-268

Edward Casey, *How to get from space to place in a fairly short stretch of time;* (Sense of Place, ed. S. Feld and K. Baso, Santa Fe, School of American Research, 1996)

Ralph Clare *Becoming Autotheory:* The Arizona Quarterly; Tucson Vol. 76, Iss. 1, (Spring 2020), pp 86-107.

Michel Certeau, *The Practice of Everyday Life;* (University of Californian Press, 1984)

Jacques Derrida, *Writing and Difference* (Routledge, 1978) p. 316.

Carl Jung, *The Tibetan Book of the Dead* ed. W.Y Evans-Wentz (Oxford University Press,1960) p. xxxvii

Fredrich Nietzsche, Twilight of the Idols; (Foulis 1911) p.6

Ben Spatz, *Blue Sky Body;* (Routledge 2020)

Harriet Tarlo (ed), *The Ground Aslant: An anthology of Radical Landscape Poetry* (Shearsman,2011)